MW01233917

Kenny's Team Unites

A Tale of Friendship & Soccer

Kathy Schanefelt

Outskirts Press, Inc.
http://www.outskirtspress.com

Paperback ISBN: 978-1-9772-3579-4
Hardback ISBN: 978-1-9772-3590-9

PRINTED IN THE UNITED STATES OF AMERICA

This book is dedicated to my mom and dad for giving me what I needed to be successful in life – their love.

Our family was blessed throughout the years as our three sons played various sports. The life lessons about respect, teamwork, practice and perseverance were invaluable. The bonds of friendship that were formed are true and lasting gifts for all of us.

Acknowledgements

Thank you to my friend Brian Beachy for sharing your remarkable talent. Several of the images in this book were adapted from Brian Beachy Photography. Thank you for allowing me to use these photos and for sharing countless photos throughout the years capturing our boys enjoying soccer and friendship.

Thank you to all our coaches through the years for your time, dedication and your focus on developing good people, not just good athletes. We are forever grateful for all those that teach, coach, lead and mentor our young people in body, mind and soul.

Thank you to my family and friends for always believing in me and loving me. A special thank you to my husband and sons for giving me the privilege of being a soccer mom.

Kenny looked at the lined fields. Lots of kids were running, juggling balls at their feet and laughing together. He wondered if he would fit in.

His momma gave him a sweet smile and told him he would do great and to have fun.

Stepping on the field he was greeted by a coach with a friendly voice, but it sounded very different than his own. Playing soccer was the first time he remembered life feeling normal since his family had moved. Being new was hard he thought, despite that Momma said he would make lots of friends.

The coach blew his whistle and Kenny lined up with all the other kids. As he looked around he saw many different faces, colors of skin, hairstyles, heights and weights.

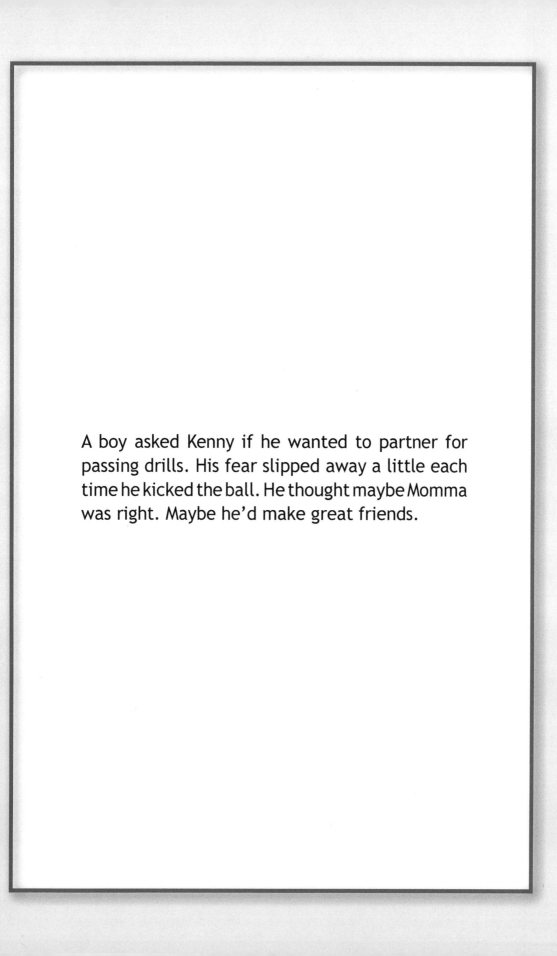

A boy asked Kenny if he wanted to partner for passing drills. His fear slipped away a little each time he kicked the ball. He thought maybe Momma was right. Maybe he'd make great friends.

As practice was ending the coach called them all into a circle. He started tossing jerseys out. He flung one Kenny's way. As he reached up to snag it, he gave a big smile. He was a part of the team. Even though he was new, and the kids all were different, they were united as a team.

The boys moved in closer to form a tight huddle. Arm in arm they chanted UNITED!

As practices continued and games started Kenny grew more comfortable. He wasn't the biggest or the fastest kid on the team, but he was getting better and he was having fun and making new friends. The boys sometimes bickered about things like video games or who would win in a game of one on one, but mostly they just laughed a lot and played soccer.

He learned about his teammates. Some had always lived in this town. Some had moved there like him, a few from other states and even a couple from other countries. Some were serious, some were funny, some were loud, and some were quiet. He liked making new friends and liked hearing about their families. He liked that they were all different, but they were all one team.

The coach talked about the importance of being a good sport, and being a good teammate. He talked about honesty, respect, integrity and working hard. He also talked about having fun.

The team practiced and improved. They won lots of games, but they also lost games too. When defeat came, they still huddled together just like that very first night. Arm in arm, they were united as a team in their wins and their losses.

Kenny not only felt like he fit in, he knew he had found something really special. He found friendship and unity in something bigger than just himself. They were a team – and every one of them was important to the team.

Kenny had found a new home in the brotherhood of his team, sharing a love of the beautiful game.

TEAM UNITED!

Jeremiah 29:11 - "For I know the plans I have for you," declares the Lord, "plans to prosper you and not to harm you, plans to give you hope and a future."

CPSIA information can be obtained
at www.ICGtesting.com
Printed in the USA
LVHW071250270221
679526LV00028B/4

* 9 7 8 1 9 7 7 2 3 5 9 0 9 *